Kayla Jensen TEDDY B-♥

The Secret Valley

The Secret Valley

Clyde Robert Bulla
Illustrated by Grace Paull

HarperTrophy
A Division of HarperCollins*Publishers*

To Bert Gray

Contents

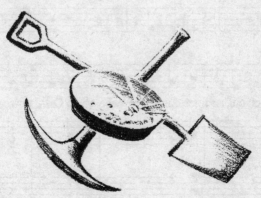

There's Gold in California

There's gold in Cal - i - for - nia, they say,—— in Cal-i-for-nia far, far a-way.—— They tell me gold is ev'ry-where. Let's hur-ry on out and get our share. We're off to Cal-i-for-nia to-day.—

I

The Wagon Train

It was early morning. The sun was not up, and the moon was shining on a cabin near the Missouri River.

There were four people inside the cabin. One was a girl eight years old. She was standing on a chair. Her father, mother, and brother stood around her while she wrote her name on the cabin wall.

1

"Ellen Davis," she wrote in big, black letters.

"Good!" said her father. "Now it's your brother's turn."

The boy took the pencil. He stood on tip-toe and wrote under his sister's name, "Frank Davis."

His mother was next. "Mary Davis," she wrote.

The man wrote his name last of all, "Henry Davis."

Then he wrote under the names, "All left for California April 26, 1849."

"When people stop here, they can read this," he said. "It will tell them we lived here and where we have gone."

He blew out the candle. They all went outside.

The wagon was ready. Hitched to it were the two mules, Spud and Spike.

"Kitty, kitty, kitty!" called Ellen, and a yellow kitten came running.

"He wants to go to California, too," said Frank.

"We can't take a cat," said Mr. Davis.

"We can't leave him here," said Ellen. "Please, let us take him."

"It's a long, hard trip to California," said Mr. Davis. "Who would take care of a cat all the way?"

"Ellen and I can take care of him," said Frank.

"He is just a little cat. See?" Ellen held the kitten up in her hands. "He won't take much room in the wagon."

"I don't think anyone ever took a cat across the West in a covered wagon," said Mr. Davis. "But if you want to try, I won't stop you."

He helped Mrs. Davis into the wagon and sat on the seat beside her. Frank and Ellen sat in the back, with the kitten between them.

"Spud—Spike—get up!" shouted Mr. Davis. The wheels turned.

"Here we go," said Frank. "We're on our way to California."

"Will we ever come back here?" asked Ellen.

"When we get to California and find gold," said Frank, "we won't want to come back."

"What if we don't find gold?" asked Ellen.

"Everyone finds gold in California," Frank told her. "Some men found it first at a place called Sutter's Mill. Then they found it in the rivers and rocks and under the trees. We'll be rich. You wait and see."

The wagon rolled along. The sky grew lighter. Birds woke up and began to sing.

"I know what I want when we get to California," said Ellen. "I want a garden."

"You had a garden here in Missouri," said Frank.

"It wasn't a good one. It was full of rocks, and the rabbits came and ate all my beans. I want a real garden, with flowers on the sides and things to eat in the middle. That's what I want in California."

"I want some land with good grass on it, so I can raise sheep and cows," said Frank. "That's what I want in California."

"Mother wants a house with a good roof and glass in the windows," said Ellen.

"And Father wants to find gold, so we can have all these things," said Frank.

He climbed over the bags and boxes to the front of the wagon. He called to Ellen, "Come and look out!"

She climbed after him. They stood behind their father and mother and looked out. They had come to a town.

"This is St. Joe," said Mr. Davis.

"Oh, look!" cried Ellen.

Back of the town was a high hill. The sun was coming up behind it. On top of the hill was a long line of covered wagons. Some had horses hitched to them. Some had mules, and others had oxen.

"Look at the people in the wagons," said Frank. "Are they going to California, too?"

"Yes," said his father. "We are all going together. We are going to help each other on the way."

They drove up the hill. A tall man in high boots came over to them.

"Here is Jim Welles," said Mr. Davis. "He is the leader."

"Hello," said Jim Welles. "Are you ready to go?"

"Yes, we are all ready," said Mr. Davis. "This is my wife."

Jim Welles took off his hat to Mrs. Davis.

"And this is my boy Frank, and here is my girl Ellen," said Mr. Davis.

Jim Welles smiled at them. "You must be the youngest two in our wagon train."

"I'm ten," said Frank, "and Ellen is eight."

"Then you are the youngest two," said Jim Welles.

"No, here is the youngest!" Ellen held up the kitten.

Jim Welles laughed. "Some of the men have dogs, but you have the only cat in the wagon train. What is his name?"

"We just call him kitty," said Frank.

"Why don't you call him Nugget?" said Jim Welles. "He looks like one."

"What is a nugget?" asked Ellen.

"A nugget is a piece of gold," Jim Welles told her, "and your cat is the color of gold."

"That's a good name," said Frank.

"I like it, too," said Ellen. "Let's call him Nugget."

Jim Welles told Mr. Davis, "Get your wagon in line. We'll soon be on our way."

Mr. Davis drove the wagon into the line. Men shouted to their horses, mules, and oxen. The wagon train began to move—west toward California.

Night on the Prairie

Night on the prai - rie, shad - ows are
fall - ing. Come to the camp - fire
where the fid-dle is call - ing.

II

Indians

The wagons rolled across Kansas. Before many days Frank and Ellen knew everyone in the wagon train.

They knew the scouts, Buck and Tony. Sometimes the scouts rode ahead to watch for Indians.

They knew Bill Miller, the boy from Illinois. He was older than they were, but he liked to play with them. At night they played hide-and-seek among the wagons, or they sat by the campfire and talked.

Ellen liked the nights best of all. The wagons were pulled up in a circle. The animals were tied where they could eat grass. The men built fires.

After supper everyone sat around the campfires. Some of the men told stories and sang songs. One man played his fiddle. Frank and Ellen wanted him to play on and on. But after a while someone would say, "Time for bed. We have to get up early in the morning."

Frank liked the nights, but he liked the days better. Every day there were new things to see. There were wolves on the prairie. There were buffalo herds.

Sometimes Buck, one of the scouts, took him for a horseback ride.

One day Buck said, "I'm going ahead to look for water. Do you want to ride with me?"

Frank climbed up behind him. They rode away.

"See those trees?" said Buck. "We may find water there."

They rode across the prairie. They stopped under the trees.

Among the trees Frank saw a high, rocky bank. Water ran out of it and into a pool below.

"It's a big spring," said Frank.

"See those tracks around the pool?" said Buck. "Wild animals come here to drink. This is their water hole."

"There is one that looks like a man's track," said Frank.

"It *is* a man's track!" said Buck.

Just then the horse jumped.

"Look!" cried Frank.

High on the bank above the pool stood an Indian. He wore only a few clothes. His face was painted green.

For a moment he stood there. Then he was gone behind the rocks.

"Hold on, Frank!" said Buck. He turned the horse around. They rode back to the wagon as fast as they could go.

"We saw an Indian," said Buck.

People called from wagon to wagon, "An Indian! They saw an Indian!"

Jim Welles told the men to drive the wagons

up in a circle. "Everyone stay inside the circle," he said. "Keep the animals inside, too. These Indians may be friendly, but load your guns and be ready."

Mr. Davis helped get the guns ready. Mrs. Davis, Frank, and Ellen got into the wagon. Frank looked out the back.

Far out on the prairie he saw something move. It was a man on a horse. Behind him came more men on horses.

Frank tried to count them. He told Ellen, "There must be fifty Indians."

Ellen looked out. "I see some with their faces painted green."

"They look like the one I saw by the water hole," said Frank. "See the man in front, on the spotted pony? He must be the chief."

"They don't have guns," said Ellen.

"No," said Frank, "but they have bows and arrows."

Close to the wagons the Indians stopped. The Indian in front held up his hand.

"Friend!" he said.

The other Indians said it, too. "Friend—friend!"

The men came out from behind the wagons. The Indians made signs to show that they wanted to trade with the white men. They had furs and horses to trade.

"No," said Jim Welles. "We have horses, and we don't need furs. But we are glad you are our friends. Will you eat with us?"

The Indians got off their horses and sat on the ground.

The women and some of the men built a fire and made coffee. They brought out ham and corn-cakes.

"Good, good!" said the Indians. They ate with both hands. They burned their mouths on the hot coffee.

Frank and Ellen stood near them. Ellen had Nugget in her arms.

An Indian boy came up to her. He patted the kitten's head. "Mew-cat," he said. He pointed to the kitten, then to his bow and arrow.

"He wants to trade his bow and arrow for your cat," said her father.

"Oh, no!" She ran away and hid Nugget in the wagon. Frank ran with her. He took his old knife out of the wagon and went back to the Indian boy.

"Will you trade your bow and arrow for this?" he asked.

The Indian boy held out his hand. He took the knife and gave Frank the bow and arrow.

When the Indians had eaten all the food, they went to their horses. As they rode away, the Indian boy looked back.

"Good-by," he said, and waved the knife.

"Good-by," said Frank, and waved the bow and arrow.

Ellen looked out of the wagon. She had Nugget in her arms. The Indian boy saw them.

"Good-by, mew-cat!" he said.

It sounded so funny that Frank and Ellen began to laugh. But the Indian boy looked sad.

Lighten the Load

Throw out the ta - ble, throw out the chair.

We've got to climb that moun-tain there throw out the horse-shoes,

leave them by the road. Now is the time to light-en the load.

III
California

Indians came out nearly every day to see the wagon train. They were friendly, and they all wanted to eat.

"If we feed them all," said Mrs. Davis, "we won't have enough food for ourselves."

But they always had food on the prairie. They had buffalo meat, and they caught fish. Once they found some wild strawberries, red and ripe and sweet.

They came to the end of the prairie. There were rivers to cross. When the water was not deep, they could drive through it. When it was deep, the men had to make a ferry-boat to take the wagons across.

Summer came, and the trail grew dry and dusty. The dust made Frank and Ellen sneeze.

Sometimes the air was full of bugs. They were big, brown bugs. They flew into the wagon. The cat patted them with his paws.

"Let's go fast," said Ellen, "and get away from the bugs."

"There are worse things than bugs," her mother told her.

Ellen found out that there *were* worse things than bugs. There were long, hot days. There were mountains to cross.

Some of the wagons were too heavy. The animals could not pull them up the mountains.

"Lighten the load!" said Jim Welles.

Up and down the wagon train, people called to each other, "Lighten the load—lighten the load!"

They threw out everything they could do without. They threw out horse-shoes and boxes and tables and chairs.

At last the animals could pull the wagons up the trail.

There was a desert to cross. There was no water on the desert. For days the wagons rolled through dust and sand.

"The sun is so hot," said Ellen. "I wish I had a drink of water."

"So do I," said Frank.

"I wish we had more water," said their father, "but the animals have to drink and we have to drink. Now the water is nearly gone."

One day Frank was riding in front with his father. Ellen and her mother and Nugget were in back of the wagon.

"Look at Spud and Spike," said Frank. "See how their ears hang down."

"The mules are tired," said his father. "They want water, too."

All at once the mules lifted their heads. Their ears stood up. They began to go faster.

"Do you know what I think?" said Mr. Davis. "I think Spud and Spike smell water."

"Can mules smell water?" asked Frank.

"Yes, and horses can, too. Sometimes they can smell water for miles."

They moved along. Ellen went to sleep in the back of the wagon. It was evening when Frank shouted, "Ellen, wake up!"

In the wagons ahead, people were shouting, "Water—water!"

Ellen sat up and looked out. There were trees ahead. There was green grass. And there was a river.

People jumped out of their wagons. They ran

to the river. They dipped water up in their hands
and drank it.

"Isn't it cool! Isn't it good!" they cried.

Frank and Ellen lay down by the water and
drank. Spud and Spike drank. All the other
animals drank.

They stayed by the river that night. They made big campfires. The fiddler got out his fiddle and played. But the best music of all was the sound of the river.

For three days they camped there. The women washed clothes and cooked. The men cut trees and made a big raft out of logs. They took the animals and wagons across the river on the raft.

After that there were more rivers. There were mountains, too.

One night the wagon train stopped on the side of a mountain. Frank and Ellen sat by their campfire.

"We've been on the road a long time," said Ellen.

"Yes," said Frank. "It was spring when we started. Now it will soon be fall."

"Nugget was a kitten when we started," said Ellen. "Now he is a big cat."

A man came out of the trees and sat down.

"Hello," he said. "Where are you from?"

"Missouri," said Frank.

"Do you live on this mountain?" asked Ellen.

"No," said the man. "I came here to find gold."

"Is there gold here?" asked Frank.

"There is gold all around us," said the man. "This is California, and the gold fields are just ahead."

Johnny Am a Lingo Lay

I came out west in the mid-dle of the year.
I like to hunt and I like to fish.

John-ny am a lin-go lay! I came out west and I
John-ny am a lin-go lay! I like to eat from an

like it here. John-ny am a lin-go lay!
old tin dish. John-ny am a lin-go lay!

IV

Father John

Some of the wagons stayed on the mountain. Some went north, some went south. Mr. and Mrs. Davis and Frank and Ellen went to a town by a river.

There were only a few houses in the town. The people called it tent city because most of them lived in tents.

People were there from all over the world. They had come to find gold, and more were coming every day.

Mr. Davis put up a tent. He cut pieces of wood for chairs and a table. Frank and Ellen brought pine branches and their mother made beds of them.

"I'm going to take the mules to a stable," said Mr. Davis.

"I'm going to the store," said Mrs. Davis. "Frank, you and Ellen stay here till we get back."

Frank and Ellen sat in the door of the tent. People went by. First there was an Indian girl. Then there were two men on a horse. They were singing a funny song.

An old man came by. He wore a big hat and a blue checked shirt. He had a white beard that came down to his belt.

"He's looking at us," said Ellen.

"He's coming over here," said Frank.

The old man came up to the tent. He smiled, and his eyes were bright. "Hello," he said.

"Hello," said Frank and Ellen.

"When did you get here?" asked the old man.

"Today," said Frank.

The man asked what their names were. They told him.

"What is your name?" asked Ellen.

The old man laughed. "People call me Father John. That's as good a name as any."

The cat put his head out of the tent.

"Bless me!" said Father John. "What's this?"

"This is our cat," said Ellen. "This is Nugget."

"Nugget?" said Father John. "How are you, Nugget?"

Nugget came out of the tent. He rubbed against Father John's boots.

"He likes you," said Frank.

Someone began to shout. Something furry and brown came running down the street.

"It's a bear!" cried Ellen.

All the hair stood up on Nugget's back. He ran and climbed high into a pine tree.

The bear went past the tent. A man ran after him. "Come back here!" he shouted.

"Don't be afraid," said Father John. "That was Pete Smith and his pet bear. Sometimes the bear runs away."

Frank went across the street. He called up the pine tree, "Nugget! You can come down now."

Nugget looked down and said, "Meow!"

People came running and stood under the tree. "It's a cat," they said "It's a cat up there!"

"Come down, Nugget!" said Frank.

"He never climbed a tree before," said Ellen. "He doesn't know how to get down."

A woman came through the crowd. She wore a pink dress and a pink bonnet. Everybody looked at her. "Is there a cat up there?" she asked.

"Yes," said Ellen. "He is our cat. We don't know how to get him down."

Pete Smith came back up the street. He had caught his pet bear. He was leading it by a rope.

"Look what you did," someone said to him. "You scared the cat up the tree."

"Did I do that?" said Pete Smith. "I'll bring him down, if someone will hold my bear."

Someone held the bear. Pete Smith took off his

boots. He climbed up the tree just like a squirrel.

"Here, kitty, kitty," he said. Everyone laughed and shouted when he picked up the cat and brought him down.

Frank and Ellen took Nugget back to the tent. Father John went with them. The woman in the pink dress went with them, too.

Father John knew her. He called her Miss Polly. "What are you doing in town?" he asked.

"I came up from the city to see my brother. I have to go back tomorrow." She said to Frank and Ellen, "Will you sell me your cat?"

"Oh, no!" said Ellen.

"If you only knew how I want a cat!" said Miss Polly. "There aren't enough cats in California, and everybody wants one."

"What for?" asked Frank.

"To keep the rats and mice away," said Miss Polly. "I have a hotel in the city. The rats and mice run all over it. A good cat would keep them away."

"We can't sell Nugget," said Frank.

"No," said Ellen. "We brought him all the way from Missouri."

"If you ever *do* want to sell him, let me know," said Miss Polly. "Good-by. Good-by, Father John."

She went away.

"Isn't she pretty?" said Ellen.

"Yes," said Father John. "She's rich, too."

"But we couldn't sell our cat," said Frank.

"Of course, you couldn't," said Father John. "Bring him to see me some day. I live in the little house by the river."

He went down the street.

"I like Father John," said Ellen.

"So do I," said Frank. "I hope we'll see him again."

With My Pick and My Shovel and My Pan

With my pick and my shov-el and my pan—— I'll start out and do the best I can. —— I'll find more gold than my hat will hold with my pick and my shov-el and my pan.—

V

Gold

In the morning Frank and his father went out to look for gold. Frank took a pan. His father took a pick and shovel.

Men were digging by the river.

"Is it all right if we dig here, too?" asked Mr. Davis.

"Yes," said one of the men, "if you can find a place."

They found a place where no one was working. Frank dug up some dirt with the pick. His father took it up in the shovel and put it into the pan.

He sat on a rock by the river. Frank stood close to him while he filled the pan with water.

Mr. Davis stirred the dirt until it was soft. He held the pan under the water and the mud washed away.

"Now only rocks are left," he said. "If there is gold, it will be under the rocks, in the bottom of the pan."

"Why?" asked Frank.

"Because the gold is so heavy," his father told him. "It is heavier than the sand or rocks."

"Do you think there is gold in this pan?" asked Frank.

"We'll soon find out." Mr. Davis took out the rocks and threw them away. He looked in the bottom of the pan. "Nothing there," he said.

They tried another pan, and another. All

the morning they worked, but they found no gold.

They went back to the tent city. Mrs. Davis and Ellen had dinner ready.

"Have you found gold?" asked Ellen.

"Not yet," said Frank.

"I hope you find some today," said Mrs. Davis. "Things cost so much at the store, we need gold to pay for them."

"I know how to pan gold now," said Frank. "I wish I had a pan."

"Could you use my wooden bowl?" asked his mother.

"I can try it," said Frank.

When he and his father went back to the river, Frank took the wooden bowl. At first they worked together. Then Frank went a little way up the river.

A man called to him, "Are you finding any gold?"

"No," said Frank.

"Look for a place where the dirt is blue," the man told him. "Blue dirt is the best for gold."

Frank found a place where the dirt was blue. He filled the bowl with dirt. He dipped the bowl into the river and washed out all the mud. One by one he picked out the rocks. In the bottom of the bowl were a few little specks. They were yellow.

He ran to his father. "I think I've found gold!"

His father looked at the yellow specks. "I think you have, too. Go to the store and show them to the man who buys gold. Ask him if this is really gold."

Frank ran to the tent city. He saw his mother and Ellen in front of the tent.

"Where are you going?" asked Ellen.

"I think I have some gold," said Frank. "I'm going to the store to find out."

"I want to go, too," said Ellen. "Please?"

"Run along, then," said Mrs. Davis.

"Come on, Ellen," said Frank. They ran through the town. People shouted at them as they went by, "Is that bowl full of gold?" Two boys and a dog began to run behind them.

Frank and Ellen ran into the store.

A man came up to them. "What can I do for you?"

Frank held out the bowl. "Will you tell me if this is gold?"

The man looked at the yellow specks. He rubbed them between his fingers. "It's gold," he said.

"Thank you," said Frank. He took Ellen's hand. "Let's go back and tell Father!"

Outside the store they met Miss Polly on a big, black horse. She was riding sidesaddle.

"Hello," she said. "Where are you going so fast?"

Frank held up the bowl. "The man says we have gold here. We are going to tell Father."

"Where is he?" asked Miss Polly.

"By the river," said Frank.

"Get on my horse," said Miss Polly. "I'll take you there."

She set Ellen in front of her. Frank got on behind, and they rode away down the trail.

"There's Father," said Ellen.

Miss Polly stopped the horse. Ellen and Frank got off.

"It *is* gold!" said Frank. "The man said so."

"Show me where you dug," said his father. "We'll dig there again." He looked at the woman on the horse. He took off his hat.

"This is Miss Polly," said Ellen. "She wanted to buy our cat."

"I still want to buy him," said Miss Polly.

"We couldn't sell Nugget," said Ellen.

"I'm sorry," said Miss Polly. "I need him to keep the rats and mice away from my hotel. I wish my little sister could see him, too."

"I didn't know you had a little sister," said Ellen.

"Yes," said Miss Polly. "She had to leave her cat back East. She is sick now, and she keeps crying for her kitty."

"Would she like to play with Nugget?" asked Frank.

"Oh, yes!" said Miss Polly. "Would you let me take him for a while? I'll give him a good home, and I'll send him back whenever you say."

Frank looked at Ellen.

"Do you want to?" he asked.

"Do *you?*" she asked.

"Miss Polly would take good care of Nugget," said Frank.

"And we can have him back when we want him," said Ellen.

"Will you let me take him with me?" asked Miss Polly.

"Yes," said Ellen.

"Oh, thank you!" said Miss Polly. She said, as she rode away, "You won't be sorry."

Mr. Davis said, "I don't think you *will* be sorry. I think you did right." He picked up his pan. "Come on. Let's see how much gold we can find to take back to your mother."

Father John's House

We know a house, a fun-ny lit-tle house half wood, half stone. And there in the house, the fun-ny lit-tle house, lives old Fath-er John all a-lone.

rit.

VI

At Father John's House

Sometimes Frank helped his father pan gold.
Sometimes he and Ellen helped their mother at
the tent. Ellen helped cook. Frank carried wood
and water.

After the work was done, there was time for
play. Frank played with two boys who lived near
him.

"I don't have anyone to play with but boys," said Ellen. "I wish a girl lived close to me."

And one day a girl came to the tent.

"May I borrow some salt?" she asked.

Mrs. Davis went to get the salt. Ellen came to the door of the tent. "Hello," she said. "Where do you live?"

"I live next door to you," said the girl. "My mother and father and I put up our tent last night. My name is Ruth."

"My name is Ellen. We came from Missouri."

"We came from San Francisco," said Ruth.

"Our cat lives in San Francisco," said Ellen.

"There's a big bay by the city," Ruth told her, "and ships are everywhere. All the sailors went to look for gold, and there's no one left to sail the ships."

Mrs. Davis gave her the salt.

"Thank you," said Ruth and went back to her tent.

"Now you have a girl to play with," Mrs. Davis said to Ellen. "She is just your size."

"Yes," said Ellen. "I'm glad she is here."

Frank came up with a load of wood. "Did you see the new people?" he asked.

"We saw the girl," said Ellen. "Her name is Ruth."

"Do you think Father John knows they are here?" asked Frank. "He goes to see all the new people."

"Let's go tell him," said Ellen. "May we go, Mother?"

"Yes, but don't stay long," said Mrs. Davis.

Frank and Ellen went through the tent city and along the river. They came to a little house that was half wood and half stone. It was Father John's house. He had made it himself.

Father John was out under the pine trees. He had on his blue checked shirt, and his long beard was white as snow.

"Hello, hello, Ellen and Frank!" he said. "Come over here and sit with me."

"We came to tell you about the new people," said Ellen.

"They came last night," said Frank.

"They have a girl named Ruth," said Ellen, "and they live in the tent by us."

"I'll go to see them," said Father John. "Maybe I can do something to help them."

"They came to look for gold," said Ellen. "Don't you ever look for gold, Father John?"

"Not very often. I don't need much."

"We need a lot," said Frank. "We want to buy some land and build a good house."

"With a garden in the back for me," said Ellen.

"And a place where I can raise sheep and cows," said Frank.

"Those are all good things," said Father John. "I hope you can have them."

"We work hard to find gold," Frank told him, "but we haven't found much yet."

"Maybe you will tomorrow," said Father John.

"That's what our father says," said Ellen.

They sat under the trees until Frank said it was time for them to go.

"I'll go with you," said Father John, "and stop to see the new people."

They walked through the tent city. From all sides, people called, "Hello, Father John," and "Where are you going?" and "When are you coming to see me?"

They all knew Father John.

That evening Frank and Ellen went to the edge of the tent city. They waited to meet their father. From the woods and the hills and the river, men were coming home. Some of them walked. Some rode horses. Some led mules that carried their packs.

Mr. Davis came out of the woods. He looked

very tired. He carried his pan and pick with him.

"Where is your shovel?" asked Frank.

"I staked a claim today," said Mr. Davis, "and I left my shovel on the claim."

"How do you stake a claim?" asked Frank.

"I found a place where I wanted to dig for gold," said Mr. Davis, "so I left my shovel there. As long as I work there and leave my shovel at night, no one else can dig there. That is the rule here."

"Did you find gold today?" asked Frank.

"No," said Mr. Davis.

"Maybe you will find gold on your claim tomorrow," said Frank. "Will you take me with you?"

"It's a long walk," said Mr. Davis, "but I'll take you tomorrow if you want to go."

"Will you let me dig?" asked Frank.

Mr. Davis laughed. "You can dig all you want to."

The Golden Land

Here in the gold-en land— There's gold in the sand of the

streams.-There's gold in the rocks, there's gold in the hills and

gold is in all our dreams.

VII

The Nugget

Frank was the first one up in the morning. He and his father took bread and meat and cheese to eat when they were hungry. They took the pick and the pan.

"We'll take the gun, too," said Mr. Davis. "Yesterday I saw a bear."

They said good-by to Mrs. Davis and Ellen. They left the tent city and started into the woods.

At first there was a trail. It was easy to follow. But soon the trail ended. They had to climb high banks. They jumped from one rock to another.

"See the marks on the trees?" said Mr. Davis. "I made them. When I follow them, I won't get lost."

They climbed a hill. They slid down the other side.

Frank saw a stream running between the rocks. He saw a hole dug by the water. In the hole was his father's shovel.

"This is my claim," said Mr. Davis.

They drank out of the stream. Then they went to work.

Frank dug up the dirt and sand. His father washed it out in the stream. All morning they worked. They found no gold.

They ate their bread and meat and cheese. Frank was glad to rest. The sun was hot, and digging the dirt was hard work.

He took off his shoes and stockings and kicked his feet in the stream. The cold water felt good on his toes.

He put on his shoes and stockings and walked down the stream. He was looking for colored rocks to take back to Ellen. Close to the water he saw something bright. It was nearly hidden in the sand.

He picked it up. At first he thought it was a rock. Then he saw that it was the color of gold.

"Father!" he cried. "*Look!*"

"What is it?" Mr. Davis ran to see. "Frank, it's gold. It's a gold nugget!" He took it in his hands. "It's bigger than a hen's egg!"

"I found it right here in the sand," said Frank.

"Let's look all around here," said Mr. Davis. "There may be more nuggets."

They looked in the sand. They looked among the rocks. For hours they looked, but they found no more gold.

"We'll look again tomorrow," said Mr. Davis.

They started home. It was dark when they got back to the tent.

"I thought you were lost," said Mrs. Davis. "Ellen and I had supper ready a long time ago." She looked tired and worried.

Mr. Davis took the nugget out of his pocket and laid it on the table.

"See what Frank found," he said.

The nugget was bright in the light of the candle. Ellen and her mother came close to it.

Ellen asked in a whisper, "Is it gold?"

"It's the biggest gold nugget I ever saw," said her father.

"Are we rich?" asked Ellen.

Her father sat down at the table. He looked at the nugget. He held it in his hand to see how heavy it was.

"We will be rich," he said. "I have a plan that will make us all rich!"

Rock the Cradle

Rock, rock, rock the cra-dle and don't stop a min-ute.— Rock, rock, rock the cra-dle with-out a ba by in it.—

VIII

At the Stream

The next day Mr. Davis showed the nugget to some men he knew. They had a meeting in the tent.

"If we can take the dirt out of the stream bed," said Mr. Davis, "we can find more gold like this."

"How can we get to the dirt?" asked one of the men.

"We can build a dam and dig a ditch by the side of it," said Mr. Davis. "The water will run down the ditch, and we can take the dirt out of the stream bed."

"That will be a lot of work," said the man.

"Yes," said Mr. Davis. "My boy and I can't do it alone. But if you will help, it won't take long. If it goes well, there will be gold for us all."

"I'll help," said the man.

"So will I," said another.

Soon all the men had told Mr. Davis they would help.

They started to work.

Frank went with them every day. He watched them dig the ditch. He helped them build the dam of mud, sticks and stones.

One day he saw a man making something out of boards and nails.

"That looks like a cradle," said Frank.

"It *is* a cradle," said the man.

"Is there a baby in the woods?" asked Frank.

"No, no!" said the man. "I'll show you how it works. You put in some dirt and pour water over it. You rock the cradle. The mud and water splash out. The gold stays in the bottom."

"May I help rock the cradle?" asked Frank.

"Yes," said the man, "if you are here tomorrow. We're going to start taking the dirt out of the stream-bed."

"I'll be here," said Frank.

Early in the morning Mr. Davis and the other men were at the dam. Frank was there, too.

Some of the men dug the dirt. Others washed it out. Mr. Davis rocked the cradle, and Frank helped him.

All morning they worked. The men looked in the pans and shook their heads. Mr. Davis looked in the bottom of the cradle and said, "No gold."

They found no gold that day or the next or the next.

At first the men had laughed and talked at their work. But after four days, they were quiet. They never laughed.

The day came when a cold wind blew. Rain began to fall.

One of the men threw down his shovel. "There's no gold here," he said. "I quit."

Another one said, "We worked hard here. Who is going to pay us?"

"Won't you try a little longer?" asked Mr. Davis.

"No," said the men. "We quit. We want our pay."

Frank said to his father, "We can sell the nugget I found. That will give us enough to pay them."

"Come to my tent tonight," Mr. Davis told the men. "I'll give you your pay."

The men went away. Frank and his father were left alone in the rain.

They stood under a tree.

"I thought we would find gold here," said Frank.

"So did I," said his father, "but your nugget must have been the only piece of gold in the stream."

"Are we going to dig here any more?" asked Frank.

"No," said Mr. Davis. "We've lost everything we worked for. We're back where we started. Let's go, Frank. Tomorrow we'll start all over again."

I'll Make You a Map

I'll make you a map. I'll show you the way to a lit-tle green val-ley I knew —— I'll make you a map. I'll show you the way to a place where your wish-es come true. ——

IX
The Map

Day after day it rained. Water ran down the streets. It leaked into the tent.

Mr. Davis tried to stop the leaks. Frank and Ellen sat with a blanket over them to keep the water off their heads. Mrs. Davis tried to cook and keep the fire going.

One day the rain stopped.

"I'd like to go outside," said Frank.

"So would I," said Ellen.

"In all this mud and water?" said their mother.

"We can walk on the rocks and jump over the water," said Frank. "We're tired of staying in the tent."

"I know you are," said Mrs. Davis. "Run along, but don't go far."

Frank and Ellen walked until they came to the river.

"It's raining again," said Ellen.

Frank took her hand. "Run! Run for Father John's house!"

They ran toward the little house. "Please let us in!" cried Ellen. "It's raining on us!"

Father John opened the door. "Bless me!" he said. "Come in!"

They nearly fell into the house. He shut the door after them.

There was only one room in the little house.

There was only one chair. Frank and Ellen sat on the bed.

The room was dry and warm. There was a fireplace, and a kettle sang over the fire.

"What have you been doing all day?" asked Father John.

"Sitting in the tent," said Ellen.

"Our father wants to go out and dig for gold," said Frank, "but he is waiting for the rain to stop."

"He hasn't had very good luck, has he?" said Father John.

"No," said Frank. "He has had bad luck."

"Why does he stay here?" asked Father John.

"Where could he go?" asked Frank.

Father John sat down at his little table. He began to draw on a piece of paper. Frank and Ellen watched him, but they could not tell what he was making.

"Is it a house?" asked Ellen.

"Is it a tree?" asked Frank

"It isn't a house and it isn't a tree," said Father John. "See? Here is a city. Here is a river. Here are mountains."

"I know," said Frank. "It's a map."

"Yes, it's a map." Father John made a mark with his pencil. "This is the tent city where we are now." He made a long line. "This is a trail. There are hills at the end of it." He made a dot with the pencil.

"What is that?" asked Ellen.

"That is a little, green valley. I call it Secret Valley, because it is hidden in the hills. Tell your father about it. In Secret Valley I think you'll find all the things you want."

When it was time for Frank and Ellen to go, it was still raining. Father John gave them an old coat. They held it over their heads and ran home through the rain.

Frank had the map in his pocket. He took it out and gave it to his father.

"This is the way to Secret Valley," he said. "Father John told us to go there."

Mr. Davis looked at the map. "It's a long way. It would take a long time to get there."

"Are we going?" asked Mrs. Davis.

"No," said Mr. Davis. "Other men have found gold here. I will, too."

"Some men have found enough gold here to make them rich," said Mrs. Davis. "Others have found only a little gold, and some have found no gold at all.''

"We'll be rich yet," said Mr. Davis. "When this rain stops, we'll go out and dig up more gold than we ever saw. Won't we, Frank?''

"We can try," said Frank.

Looking for a Letter

We're look-ing for a let-ter. What makes the mail so slow? We wrote to San Fran-cis-co a long time a-go.

X

A Letter to Miss Polly

All winter long, more people came to the tent city. They came in wagons and on horseback. They came on foot. The tent city was a crowded, noisy place.

The people next door to the Davis tent moved away.

"Now I won't have Ruth to play with any more," said Ellen.

"I wish we could go away, too," said Mrs. Davis.

"So do I," said Ellen. "This tent is always wet and cold."

"And when we have a little gold, it all goes to buy food and clothes," said Mrs. Davis. "Your father says if he doesn't find more gold soon, we *will* go away."

Ellen told Frank, "Father says we may go away from here."

"I hope we go soon," said Frank, "and I hope we go to Secret Valley."

Ellen looked worried. "What about our cat?"

"What about him?" asked Frank.

"If we go away, Miss Polly won't know where to send him."

"She told us we could have him back when we wanted him," said Frank. "Let's write her a letter."

They found a paper bag and cut it in two. Ellen made an envelope of one half. Frank wrote on the other half.

Dear Miss Polly:

Will you please send back our cat, Nugget? We may go away from here, and we want to take him with us.

Your friends,

FRANK & ELLEN DAVIS

They mailed the letter in the post office at the store.

They waited a week. After that they went to the store every day. They asked the man at the post office, "Do you have a letter for us? Has our cat come from San Francisco?"

Always the man said no.

"Maybe Miss Polly didn't get our letter," said Ellen.

"Maybe she went away and took Nugget with her," said Frank.

While they waited, the days grew warmer. The snow on the mountains began to melt.

Mrs. Davis said one day, "Can't we move our tent? Every time we go outside we step in the mud."

"Yes, and horses and mules run up and down the street," said Ellen. "Yesterday a horse put his head into our tent when I was eating my dinner. He made me drop my dish."

"I know a place just outside the city," said Mr. Davis. "It's close to the river. We can set up our tent on the sand."

They moved the tent. They made new beds of pine branches.

"This is better," said Mrs. Davis.

They went to bed early. The sound of the river put them to sleep.

In the middle of the night Frank woke up. His feet were cold and wet. He put his hand outside the bed. There was water all over the floor, and more was running into the tent.

"Get up, get up!" he shouted. "It's a flood!"

They all jumped up. They bumped into each other in the dark. They ran outside.

"Let's save all we can!" said Mrs. Davis.

They splashed through the water and took nearly everything out of the tent. They took down the tent. They carried everything to a high place.

"What made the water come up?" asked Frank.

"I think it was the snow melting in the mountains," said Mrs. Davis. She sat down on a rock and told Frank and Ellen to sit by her. "We'll keep each other warm," she said.

Mr. Davis sat down on the rock, too. His clothes were wet. There was water in his boots.

"I'm ready to leave this place," he said. "Who wants to go with me?"

"I do," said Mrs. Davis.

"I do, too," said Ellen.

"So do I," said Frank.

"Then we'll go," said Mr. Davis. "We'll go in the morning."

When the sun came up they went to the stables. The wagon was there. The mules were there, too.

"Where are we going?" asked Frank.

"To Father John's valley," said Mr. Davis. "Maybe our luck will be better there."

"We want to say good-by to Father John," said Ellen.

"Go over to his house, then," said Mr. Davis, "while I hitch Spud and Spike to the wagon."

Frank and Ellen went to Father John's house.

"We came to say good-by," said Ellen.

"We're going to Secret Valley," said Frank.

"Bless me!" said Father John. "I'll miss you, but I'm glad you are going to Secret Valley."

"I wish you were going, too," said Ellen.

"Maybe some day I will go," he said. "If I do, I hope I'll see you there."

"We hope so, too," said Ellen. "And Father John, if Miss Polly sends our cat back, will you take care of him for us?"

"I'll be glad to," said Father John.

He said good-by. Frank and Ellen said good-by. The last they saw of him, he was in front of his little house, waving to them.

In the middle of the tent city, Ellen stopped. "Let's go to the post office. Maybe there is a letter from Miss Polly."

They went to the post office. "We are going away today," Ellen told the man. "We would like to have a letter before we go."

"There's no letter for you," said the man.

They went back to the stables. Spud and Spike were hitched to the wagon.

Frank and Ellen sat in the back. Their father and mother sat in the front. They rode away.

Just outside the tent city, Frank and Ellen saw a man riding a horse down the road. He was coming fast. He had a box under his arm.

"Are you Frank and Ellen Davis?" he called.

"Yes, sir," they said.

"I have a box for you. It just came on the stage-coach. They told me at the post office that you were going away, and I came to catch you." The

man gave them the box. He turned his horse around and rode back toward the tent city.

Frank and Ellen looked at the box. It was a pretty box made of wood and painted red and black. There were holes in the top.

"Shall we open it?" asked Ellen.

"He said it was for us," said Frank.

They opened the box.

"Oh!" cried Ellen.

Out jumped something big and soft and yellow.

"It's a cat!" cried Frank. "It's Nugget!"

"Meow!" said the cat.

"Miss Polly did get our letter! She did send you back!" said Ellen.

"Don't be afraid, Nugget," said Frank.

"You don't have to ride in a box any more." Ellen put the box out of sight in the wagon.

"He knows us now," said Frank.

"Of course, he does. This is like the day we left the cabin in Missouri. Do you remember, Frank?

We rode in the back of the wagon with Nugget."

"Only he was a kitten then. Now he is a big cat.
Aren't you, Nugget?"

And Nugget curled up between them and
began to purr.

The Deer

Out of the woods, on a night in spring, came a
lit-tle brown deer a-lone.— He looked at the moon and he
looked at the stars, and the val-ley was all his own.

XI

The Secret Valley

They drove south, through woods and across streams. Every night they looked at Father John's map. Every day they came a little nearer to Secret Valley.

At last they could see the hills Father John had marked on his map. A trail led into the hills.

They followed the trail. They climbed higher and higher.

Mr. Davis called back to Frank and Ellen, "We are nearly to the top."

Frank and Ellen went to the front of the wagon.

"Whoa!" said Mr. Davis, and the mules stopped on top of the hill.

Far below was Secret Valley. It was green with grass and trees. Flowers were in bloom on the hills. A stream ran out of the hills and across the valley, and the water was bright as silver.

"Isn't it beautiful!" said Ellen.

They went down into the valley. They drank from the stream. The mules drank, too. Nugget jumped out of the wagon and rolled on the grass.

"It's quiet here," said Frank.

It was so quiet they could hear birds singing a long way off. They could hear water running over the rocks.

Frank and his father put up the tent. When night came, Mrs. Davis said, "It's time to go to bed."

But no one wanted to go to bed. They sat outside the tent and looked at the moon and stars. The moon had never looked so big to them before. The stars had never looked so bright.

A deer came out of the woods. He came so close they could see his soft, dark eyes. He stood and looked at the sky, then he went quietly away.

"Wasn't he beautiful!" said Ellen.

"Everything is beautiful here," said her mother.

They went to bed late, but they got up early in the morning.

"Come, Frank," said Mr. Davis, "let's see how much gold we can find."

They took the pick, shovel, and pan to the stream. They worked all day and washed out pan after pan of dirt. They found only rocks and sand.

The next day they tried again. Frank and his father worked up and down the stream. Again they found no gold.

The third day, while they worked, a man came across the valley. He was leading a mule with a pack on its back. He called to Mr. Davis and Frank, "What are you doing there?"

"Looking for gold," said Mr. Davis.

"Gold?" said the man. "There's no gold here."

"How do you know?" asked Mr. Davis.

"Lots of men have looked, and nobody ever found gold here," said the man. "I am on my way up north. That's where the gold is."

He went away. Mr. Davis sat with his head in his hands.

"We came all the way to this valley," he said, "and there's no gold."

"What are we going to do?" asked Frank.

"What is there to do," said his father, "but go back to the tent city?"

We Found Gold

We found gold in our val-ley—Just as bright as the
gold at Sut-ter's mill—There's gold in the Cal-i-for-nia
sun-shine—and gold in the pop-pies on the hill.—

XII

Gold in California

Frank and his father went to the tent. They put down the pick, shovel and pan.

"What's the matter?" asked Mrs. Davis.

"There's no gold here," said Mr. Davis.

Ellen was under the trees, playing with Nugget. When she saw her father and Frank, she came to the tent. "Did you find gold?" she asked.

"There's no gold here," said Frank.

"But Father John told us to come here," said Ellen. "We aren't going away, are we?"

"You want to find gold, don't you?" asked Mr. Davis.

"Yes," said Ellen, "but I wish we could find it here."

"So do I." Mr. Davis went to the wagon. "We'll get ready, so we can go in the morning."

"Where are we going?" asked Mrs. Davis.

"Back to the gold country." Mr. Davis took the mules' harness out of the wagon. A red and black box came out with it.

"Miss Polly sent our cat back in that box," said Frank. He took the box.

"Isn't it pretty?" said Ellen. "We never had a good look at it before."

Frank shook the box. "There's something in it."

He set it down. He and Ellen looked inside it.

"Here is a little leather bag!" cried Ellen.

"With a letter tied to it!" said Frank.

He opened the letter. It was from Miss Polly.
He read it to his sister.

Dear Frank and Ellen:

I am sending Nugget back, as you asked me to do. He is a fine cat. He has kept the rats and mice away. My little sister is well now. She played with Nugget every day. I am sending a gift to show how thankful I am.

Ellen opened the leather bag. "I see something bright," she said. "It looks like gold!"

It *was* gold. There were little nuggets. There was gold dust. Mr. Davis poured some of it into his hand, and it sparkled in the sun.

"What are you going to do with this gold?" he asked.

"Is there enough to buy some land?" asked Frank.

"Yes," said his father.

"Would there be enough land for me to have a garden?" asked Ellen.

"Yes," said her father.

"And we could have a house on the land," said Mrs. Davis. "We could have it here in this valley."

"Yes!" said Frank.

"Yes!" said Ellen. "Here in this valley!"

"Maybe Father John was right," said Mr. Davis. "He said if we came here we could find what we want. I thought he meant gold. Now I think he meant something better than gold."

"We could cut some trees and build a cabin," said Mrs. Davis.

"I could have my garden," said Ellen.

"The grass is good here," said Frank. "I could raise sheep and cows."

"Then we'll stay in this valley," said Mr. Davis. "Long after the gold in California is gone, the land will be here, and this land will be ours."

"There is more than one kind of gold," said Mrs. Davis. "Look—there is gold in the flowers on the hill."

"There's gold in the sunshine all around us," said Frank.

"And Nugget is gold, too," said Ellen. She picked up the cat and held him in her arms.